NINA
AND THE MAGICAL CARNIVAL

Madhvi Ramani

Illustrated by Erica-Jane Waters

Tamarind

NINA AND THE MAGICAL CARNIVAL
A TAMARIND BOOK 978 1 848 53092 8

First published in Great Britain by Tamarind Books,
an imprint of Random House Children's Publisher's UK
A Penguin Random House Company

Penguin
Random House
UK

This edition published 2014

1 3 5 7 9 10 8 6 4 2

The Random House Group Limited supports the Forest Stewardship Council (FSC®), the
leading international forest-certification organisation. Our books carrying the FSC label are
printed on FSC®-certified paper. FSC is the only forest certification scheme supported by
the leading environmental organisations, including Greenpeace.
Our paper procurement policy can be found at www.randomhouse.co.uk/environment

MIX
Paper from
responsible sources
FSC® C016897

Set in Bembo Mt Schoolbook 13/20pt

Tamarind Books are published by Random House Children's Publishers UK,
61–63 Uxbridge Road, London W5 5SA

www.tamarindbooks.co.uk
www.randomhousechildrens.co.uk
www.randomhouse.co.uk

Addresses for companies within The Random House Group Limited
can be found at: www.randomhouse.co.uk/offices.htm

THE RANDOM HOUSE GROUP Limited Reg. No. 954009

A CIP catalogue record for this book is available from the British Library.

Printed and bound by CPI Group (UK) Ltd, Croydon, CR0 4YY

For Isha

Chapter One

"Now, pretend you are an animal," Madame Celeste told the class.

Nina tried not to groan. *Was this lesson ever going to end?*

Her drama teacher had dark wavy hair, caramel skin and green eyes. She walked around the classroom looking at what everyone was doing.

Simon barked and growled: a dog. Tanya stuck out her front teeth and twitched her nose:

a rabbit. Sita prowled the floor on all fours, roaring at the other animals: a lion.

The beads around Madame Celeste's neck clacked as she moved towards Nina.

Nina tried to think of an animal. A zebra? She needed stripes for that. A hedgehog? She didn't have any spikes. A bird! Nina flapped her arms, wishing she really were a bird and could fly right out of the classroom. She bet she looked nothing like a bird. She didn't feel like one. She felt silly.

After the lesson Madame Celeste called her name. Nina turned round with dread. Was Madame Celeste going to tell her off for the awful bird impression?

"Nina, what are you doing for the talent show?" said Madame Celeste, looking at her list. Beside the names of Nina's classmates were descriptions of what they would be doing in the show. Next to Nina's name was a blank space.

Simon Davies: Clown act
Luca Melissi: Juggling
Nina Raja:
Tanya Spalding: Ballet

"Um, I need some more time to think about it," said Nina.

"But it is Tuesday already, and the talent show is this Friday. Students, teachers and parents are all going to be there," said Madame Celeste.

"I know," said Nina. "That's why I have to think about it carefully. Whatever I do has to be . . . perfect."

Madame Celeste's green eyes glittered. "Ah, I see. You are always the best at everything you do. But it is hard to be perfect all the time. To be creative, your mind must be free. Like a bird," she said, flinging out her arms. Her body seemed to rise. Her bracelets and beads danced. "You need a *fantasia*," she whispered. The word

sounded funny and magical: fan-ta-see-ah.

"Cool. What's that?" said Nina.

"In Brazil, where I grew up, the word *fantasia* has many meanings. For example, it is a costume that you wear at Carnival."

Nina nodded. She had seen a TV programme about Brazil. It was a country in South America. Every year it celebrated Carnival – a festival of music and dancing, costumes and masks. In fact, the carnival was happening right now.

"A costume – a normal *fantasia* – can help you become something else. But I'm talking about a special *fantasia*, one that can help you become *anything* in the world. Every single person has one – you just need to find yours. It is a *fantasia* for up here," said Madame Celeste, swirling her hands around her head.

Nina recalled the feathered headdresses she had seen on TV.

"Right . . ." she said. How was she going

to find a special *fantasia* for her head in rainy old England? What she needed were some rules to follow. Like in maths, where you could learn them and get the right answer every time. "Maybe you could just give me homework or something?"

"Homework? Ah, of course! My homework for you, Nina, is to be spontaneous. Don't think too much. Just let yourself go!"

Chapter Two

Well, that wasn't very helpful, thought Nina as she walked home. Still, homework was homework. Besides, she couldn't stand up in front of everyone on Friday and do nothing. That would be embarrassing. People would laugh, or boo. Her parents and teachers would be disappointed.

Be spontaneous! Madame Celeste had said. *Fine*, thought Nina, and she turned left onto Aunt Nishi's road instead of continuing straight home.

Nina loved going to her aunt's house. She especially loved the garden shed where Aunt Nishi stored her spices. It was no ordinary shed. It was a travelling machine that could take you anywhere in the world in an instant! Nina imagined using it to escape to Florida, where she could lounge on the beach until the talent show was over . . .

She sighed as she walked up the path to Aunt Nishi's house. Her aunt would never allow her to miss school.

She pressed the doorbell. Aunt Nishi opened the door wearing a lime-green shalwar kameez

patterned with orange mangoes. Her silver curls bounced around her head. She looked like a normal Indian auntie, but just like the shed in her garden, there was more to her than met the eye.

"It's my favourite niece!" said Aunt Nishi.

"I'm your only niece," Nina pointed out.

Aunt Nishi was a computer whizz who worked for the government, although no one in Nina's family knew exactly what she did. As Nina entered the house, she thought about all the times she had asked her aunt about her job. Somehow, Aunt Nishi always managed to dodge her questions.

In the living room, Milo, Aunt Nishi's robotic dog, wagged his tail when he saw Nina. The room was cluttered with piles of books, Japanese fans, African carvings and peculiar gadgets. Nina picked up a metal bowl with multi-coloured rods and wires sticking out of it.

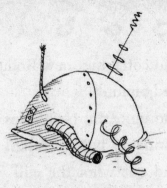

"What's this?" she asked.

"My thinking cap," said Aunt Nishi.

Nina was about to ask how it worked when a shrill ringing interrupted her. Aunt Nishi dashed to the kitchen with Milo at her heels. Nina had heard that sound before. It was the special phone in the kitchen. The one Nina wasn't allowed to touch.

Aunt Nishi's phone call reminded Nina that she had a call of her own to make. She picked up the regular phone and dialled home.

"I'm paying Aunt Nishi a spontaneous visit," she said to her mum.

"How nice!" said her mum. "Maybe your dad and I will do something spontaneous too . . . In fact, if we leave now, we might

just be able to catch that new Bollywood film in town. See you later!"

Nina hung up. Aunt Nishi was still in the kitchen, talking in hushed tones. Nina was dying to find out what the call was about, but she didn't want to snoop. Instead, she practised being spontaneous. She did a spontaneous walk, bending her knees and swinging her arms in a funny fashion. She spontaneously tapped some keys on a laptop. The words TOP SECRET MISSION and a picture of a crown came up. She quickly shut the lid. She spontaneously picked up the thinking cap and put it on.

Aunt Nishi burst back in with Milo.

"Nina, I'm afraid I have to work tonight. You'll have to go home. I'm so sorry, I'll make it up to you."

"But I think Mum and Dad have gone to the cinema," said Nina.

Aunt Nishi rang Nina's house. There was

no answer. Then she tried calling Nina's mum and dad on their mobile phones. Nobody picked up.

"Oh dear. They must be at the cinema already and I've got an emergency in Rio. I don't suppose you could stay here by yourself, not with all my . . ." Aunt Nishi glanced at her government papers and gadgets. "No, that won't do at all," she continued as Milo nudged her leg with his nose: he wanted her to get a move on.

Aunt Nishi might have run out of ideas, but Nina's head was buzzing with them. "Rio" was short for Rio de Janeiro, the city in Brazil where the biggest carnival in the world was taking place! Nina remembered what Madame Celeste had said about finding her *fantasia*. If she could find a magical *fantasia* for her head in Brazil, she could become whatever she wanted for the talent show: a singer, a magician, a clown . . .

11

"I'll come with you!" said Nina.

"Come with me, to Rio? Out of the question," replied Aunt Nishi.

"Maybe I could help," said Nina, thinking she might be able to find out more about Aunt Nishi's job as well.

Aunt Nishi frowned.

"Come on, Auntie. I can look after myself. After all, I've travelled to India and China before. I won't get in the way, and I'll do whatever you say." For added effect, Nina made her eyes big and wide. It was a trick she had picked up from a street boy in India, who swore it always made adults give you what you wanted.

Aunt Nishi looked at her. "Well, I suppose you *are* well-behaved . . ." she admitted as Milo grabbed the bottom of her shalwar kameez and tugged her towards the door. "But you'd better take off that thinking cap. It's conspicuous," she said.

Nina took the cap off. She wondered if it was responsible for her quick thinking. Then she tossed it aside – she was going to Brazil!

Chapter Three

Nina and Aunt Nishi tramped through the overgrown garden towards the spice shed. It was getting dark. Fog hung in the air. Nina could hardly see the crooked old shed at the bottom of the garden. She was bursting with questions, but she kept quiet. She wanted to prove that she wouldn't cause any trouble. After all, Aunt Nishi could still change her mind.

Nina had not put a foot wrong so far. In the house, she had changed her watch to Brazilian time, as she had seen Aunt Nishi do. She had inspected the Brazilian money that her aunt had given her, just in case. The notes were green, purple and yellow and said *1 Real*, *5 Reals* and *20 Reals* on them. Nina had carefully tucked the money away in her pocket. Finally, while Aunt Nishi had stuffed her bag with laptops and gadgets, Nina had picked up her notepad and pen and made a To Do list.

To Do in Brazil:
1. Find out more about Aunt Nishi's job.
2. Help Aunt Nishi.
3. Find a special fantasia for my head.

At the shed, Aunt Nishi unlocked the door with the tiny gold key hanging from her necklace. The lock clicked. Aunt Nishi pushed the door open and they stepped inside. A light flickered on and the door swung shut behind them. Nina's nose twitched at the smell of cinnamon and cloves, paprika and pepper.

Jars of different-coloured spices lined shelves along two sides of the shed. A Mexican sombrero, scuba-diving equipment, skis and other bits and bobs were piled against the back wall. Nina could see the broomstick peeking out among them. Aunt Nishi grabbed

it and pulled. It swung forward like a lever.

A low whining sound filled the shed as a flat screen slid down from the ceiling. On it glowed a map of the world, and the words:

TOUCH SCREEN TO GO TO DESTINATION

"You can do the honours," said Aunt Nishi.

Nina raised her finger and touched Rio de Janeiro on the map. The shed began to shake. Nina grabbed a shelf to keep her balance. The jars of spices rattled and clinked. Tiny multi-coloured particles whizzed about in the air.

"Must . . ." said Aunt Nishi as she hopped about to keep her balance, "do . . . something . . . about—"

Suddenly everything went still.

". . . the suspension on this thing," finished Aunt Nishi.

Nina looked at the screen. The words now read:

WELCOME TO RIO DE JANEIRO, BRAZIL

She pushed the door open.

Chapter Four

Nina stepped out onto the rocky soil. It was warm. Tall bushes with rubbery leaves surrounded her. Nina peeked through them. On the other side, people walked along a path, carrying cameras. They looked like tourists. At the top of the path, a gigantic white statue of a man with his arms stretched out rose into the blue sky.

"That's Christ the Redeemer," whispered Aunt Nishi. "Come on, we need to get out of here without drawing attention."

The tourists were so busy taking photos of the statue that they didn't notice Aunt Nishi and Nina sneak out of the shrubbery. From the path, Nina could see they were high up, atop a mountain. The entire city sprawled out below, all the way to the sparkling sea.

Aunt Nishi started marching down the path away from the statue. Nina remembered that they were here on business: she took out her notepad and pen, and followed.

"So, what are we doing here?" asked Nina.
"Looking for something," said Aunt Nishi.
"What?"

"Something valuable," her aunt replied mysteriously.

Nina thought about the picture of the crown that had popped up on Aunt Nishi's computer. Aunt Nishi clearly didn't want to tell her any more, so Nina tried a different approach.

"Where are we going?"

"You'll see," said Aunt Nishi.

"You should probably tell me. I mean, what should I do if we get separated?" said Nina.

"Good point. If that happens, I'll meet you back at the shed at 19.00 hours. You can hardly lose it – Christ the Redeemer can be seen for miles around," said Aunt Nishi, pointing up at the massive statue.

Nina wrote that down as she hurried after her aunt.

At the bottom of the path, they jumped into a yellow taxi. Aunt Nishi said something in another language to the driver.

"I didn't know you could speak Brazilian," said Nina.

"Brazilian's not a language. Here, they speak Portuguese," replied Aunt Nishi.

"Oh," said Nina.

"But I can speak English if you like," said the taxi driver, smiling at Nina in the rear-view mirror. "Also Spanish, French, Italian, German . . ."

"Wow, that's a lot of languages," said Nina.

"Yes, I get passengers from all over the world in my taxi," continued the man. "I'm Ronaldo, like the football player. He's Ronaldo the greatest football player in the world, and I'm Ronaldo the greatest taxi driver in the world!"

"Right," said Nina. She didn't want to admit that she hadn't heard of Ronaldo the football player. Ronaldo the taxi driver, however, was excellent. He was fast, friendly and stopped at all the red lights in time.

"On the left is Ipanema beach," he said, braking in a line of traffic. Car horns tooted.

"We'd better walk from here," said Aunt Nishi.

"Call me if you need a taxi," said Ronaldo, holding out his card. Nina put it in her pocket as she got out, and sniffed the salty air.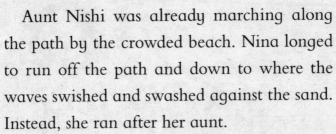

Aunt Nishi was already marching along the path by the crowded beach. Nina longed to run off the path and down to where the waves swished and swashed against the sand. Instead, she ran after her aunt.

"Keep up. Don't draw attention to yourself and wait where I tell you," said Aunt Nishi.

On the beach, people chatted, laughed and played ball games. Vendors walked around selling sunglasses, sweets, matches, hats and food.

"Hayal! Hayal!" they shouted. Nina wondered what it meant. She looked to see if anyone was selling feathered headdresses. How would she know when she discovered her very own special *fantasia*?

As she scanned the beach, Nina saw something that made her stop: a crying girl, searching the sand and looking lost. She seemed out of place among all the other

relaxed, happy people. Nina started walking towards her, wanting to help, but then she suddenly remembered Aunt Nishi. She turned back towards the path, and her heart skipped a beat. Aunt Nishi was nowhere in sight!

Nina hunted for a flash of lime green or a mango-shaped pattern in the crowd. She felt as if she were lost in a strange sea. She searched the bobbing heads, but she couldn't see even one bouncy silver curl.

Then Nina spotted the statue of Christ the Redeemer, high above everything. She checked her notes. If they got separated, they would meet back at the shed, near the statue, at 19.00 hours. She relaxed a bit. She had plenty of time and money to get back to their meeting place, even though she dreaded to think what Aunt Nishi would say when she got there. Nina had persuaded her aunt to bring her along, only to let her down.

Nina turned back to the girl on Ipanema beach. Maybe they could be lost together for a bit, she thought, and went over.

Chapter Five

"Are you OK?" asked Nina.

The girl looked up. She had golden skin, wavy hair and light brown eyes.

"No, I am not. My *fantasia* is ruined and I must dance in the samba parade in one hour!" she said. A new set of tears filled her eyes.

A *fantasia*? That's what Nina needed! But what was the samba parade? Nina asked the girl.

"You have not heard of it? It is an important part of Carnival. Samba is a dance, and every year more than two hundred samba schools try to put on the most fantastical

parade at a big place called the Sambadrome. Thousands of people come to watch."

Nina thought it sounded a bit like the talent show, although this seemed like a much bigger deal.

"But now your costume's ruined, you've got the perfect excuse to get out of it!" she said.

"Get out of it? Carnival is when I have the most fun! Why would I want to get out of it?"

Nina shrugged. She didn't understand why the girl was so keen to take part, but she knew how worrying it was to be unprepared for an upcoming show.

"Can I do something to help?" asked Nina.

"I need shells like this to fix my costume," said the girl, holding up a white, fan-shaped shell.

Nina knelt down next to her. She sifted through the fine white sand, and tossed aside a plastic straw, pebbles, tangled bits of

seaweed and broken shells. She found a pink cone-shaped shell, and a speckled black and white one. Finally she discovered a white shell like the one the girl had shown her.

"Here," said Nina. The girl smiled, and held out her bag, which was half full. Nina dropped it in. It clinked as it joined the others.

As they moved along the beach, the clinks came more often and the two girls chatted away. Nina found out that the girl's name was Fernanda, and that her entire family had put their money together to help buy her *fantasia*.

"Wow. It must be expensive. Is it a special *fantasia*?" asked Nina.

"Yes, very special. I cannot dance in the parade without it," said Fernanda.

"I think I know what you mean. I've got a show on Friday and I'm in trouble unless I find a special *fantasia* for my head."

"Oh, you mean a *fantasia de cabeça*. That is what we call it in Portuguese."

"Yes, but how do you find your special one? What should it look like?" asked Nina.

"Well, it should be very beautiful. And it should fit," said Fernanda.

"Is that all?" asked Nina. "Does it make you feel different when you wear it? Like you can be anything in the world?"

Fernanda's eyes sparkled. "Yes, that is exactly how it feels," she said.

Nina dropped another shell into the bag – it was full now.

"Let's go!" said Fernanda.

They hurried off the beach and ran up a hill, past some tall apartment blocks and glitzy hotels. Then they turned into a narrow street and everything changed: the buildings became smaller, more crowded together, and were unpainted.

Fernanda ran into one of the buildings, and a little boy came running out, kicking a football. Fernanda shouted and tried to grab him, but he was too fast. He kicked the ball straight through Nina's legs as she followed Fernanda inside, and then he continued to dribble it up the road, out of sight.

"That is my brother, Oscar. He spoiled my costume. He thinks he is Ronaldo," said Fernanda, rolling her eyes. "This is my baby brother Carlos, and my mother," she said, introducing a toddler who was banging a pot with a spoon, and a woman who was cooking something that smelled delicious. She looked lovely, like an older version of Fernanda.

Fernanda's *fantasia* hung from a hook on the wall. It was made of white shells, but there was a football-shaped patch in the middle, where a bunch had fallen off. A pile of broken shells had been swept into a corner. Fernanda's mum started fixing the new shells on as soon as her daughter gave her the bag.

Fernanda paced up and down. Only half an hour remained before her samba school was due to perform. Nina tried to take her mind off it.

"Why don't you show me your dance?" said Nina.

"OK. But not here," said Fernanda, and led Nina up some stairs to the roof. It was flat

and spacious. Clothes flapped on a washing line.

"This is where I practise the samba, after I finish my schoolwork and chores," said Fernanda. She began to dance. For the first time that day, Nina saw Fernanda smile. She seemed to sway like the waves in the distance behind her.

"Fernanda!" came a shout from below.

Fernanda stopped dancing and ran down

the stairs. Before following, Nina took one last look over the patchwork of rooftops. She spotted Oscar in the street below. He bounced his ball from one knee to another, then up to his head and down to his ankle. If she could do *that*, she would be the star of the talent show.

Downstairs, Fernanda tried on the costume. Not a single shell was missing, but Fernanda looked crestfallen.

"I only have fifteen minutes to get to the Sambadrome. I will never make it," she said.

"Don't worry. I know someone who might be able to help," said Nina, taking Ronaldo's card out of her pocket.

Chapter Six

The taxi screeched to a halt in front of the Sambadrome. Ronaldo had taken every short cut he knew to get them there quickly. Nina looked at her watch. They had three minutes to spare.

"Can you meet me back here in two hours?" asked Nina. All this rushing about had reminded her of another important deadline – meeting Aunt Nishi at the shed. She wondered how Aunt Nishi's mission was going, and whether she had found the valuable object she'd been looking for.

"Sure. You're becoming a regular customer!" said Ronaldo.

Fernanda and Nina entered the Sambadrome. The sound of drums shook the air. Crowds cheered and waved flags from the stalls. In the middle of the stadium was a long strip, like a runway. Wild animals strutted down it in time with the music. Of course, they weren't *real* animals, but performers

wearing costumes. The giraffes were people on stilts who swayed their long necks to the beat of the drums. The ostriches were girls wearing black and white feathery skirts, which swelled as they twirled. The lions wore feathered headpieces that looked like manes. There must have been over a thousand people in that samba school's parade!

"Every samba school has a different theme," shouted Fernanda above the noise. "Theirs is Africa."

"Cool. What's your school's theme?" asked Nina as they entered a backstage area. A woman seized Fernanda before she could answer. A massive float shaped like a blue whale filled the room. People in seahorse and starfish costumes ran about, putting on a last dash of make-up or adjusting their costumes as they prepared for their school's parade to start. Nina guessed that their theme was the sea.

There were feathered headpieces every-where. Hundreds of them! How was Nina ever going to find her special one? They were all very beautiful, which didn't help narrow it down, and she could hardly try on each one to see if it fitted and made her feel different.

Nina noticed that Fernanda and the woman were gesturing at her. The woman looked stressed out. Nina wasn't surprised. How was all this chaos going to be turned into a fantastic parade?

Fernanda turned to Nina. "One of the girls is sick and we need someone to take her place," she said.

"Oh no . . ." said Nina, guessing what was coming next. She had been looking forward to sitting back and watching the parade, not taking part in it!

"Please, there is not much time," said Fernanda as a woman holding a huge flag started to twirl and inch towards the arena.

Her multi-coloured dress fanned out around her. It glinted as if made of a thousand fish scales. She stepped out into the lights. The parade had begun!

Nina shook her head.

"All you have to do is be a wave," said Fernanda, pointing to a group of girls in glittery blue cloaks and feathered headdresses. The woman held out a matching costume for Nina.

Mists of spray started to puff out of the whale's blowhole as it rolled onto the strip after the flag bearer. Cheers rose from the crowds.

The headdress was made of long blue and white feathers. It glittered and looked like a crashing wave. Nina wanted to try it on. After all, this could be her special *fantasia*.

The whale float was now rolling down the strip, pulling a string of giant oyster shells behind it. Men and women dressed in *fantasias* made of pearls danced in each one.

Fernanda begged Nina with pleading eyes. The woman looked like she was going to explode from stress. Nina weighed it up: if this was her special *fantasia*, she would have no problem being a wave. On the other hand . . .

Fernanda ran to join a group of girls with costumes made out of shells, like hers. It was their turn to join the parade now. As they started to dance after a group of drummers, their shells clicked and clacked.

Madame Celeste's voice echoed in Nina's head: *Don't think too much. Just let yourself go!*

Nina reached out and took the *fantasia de cabeça*. The woman draped the glittery cloak around her. Nina raised the *fantasia de cabeça* to her head. She put it on. It fitted!

Nina joined the other waves. Her body tingled. She hoped the feeling was because of

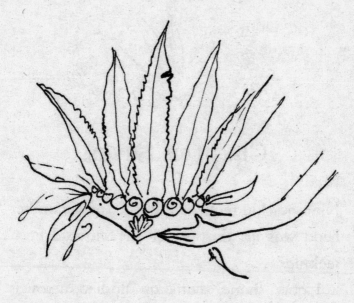

her *fantasia*, giving her the power to become anything in the world, and not her nerves. Then she was swept out into the lights.

Chapter Seven

Nina quickly realized that the *fantasia* on her head was *not* the special one she had been seeking.

Lights shone, cameras flashed, crowds cheered . . . and Nina shuffled about. She had no idea what she was doing! Everyone around her sparkled. They smiled and moved to the beat.

"Oh! . . . Ouch! . . . Oops!"

Nina stepped on the toes of the other waves. The girls just behind had to push her forwards so she wouldn't hold up the rest of the parade. She wanted to run away, but dancers and drummers surrounded her.

TV cameras swooped around them, and big screens all over the stadium showed different parts of the parade. She was trapped.

She tried to copy the other waves. They quick-stepped while their arms circled, torsos twisted, hips swayed and heads turned left and right – it was too much!

Right, thought Nina, *I'll concentrate on my feet first.*

One-two-three, one-two-three . . .

But she was always a step behind. The feathers on her headdress drooped and got in the way of the other girls as she studied everyone's feet. Nina stood out more than ever. She grew hot with frustration.

She tried to think back to when Fernanda had showed her the samba on the roof, but her mind was blank.

A mist of spray from the whale's blowhole drifted her way. It sprinkled her with cool, salty water. Suddenly Nina remembered

how Fernanda seemed to move like waves when she danced. If Nina could figure out how a wave moved, she could figure out the dance!

But what did one single wave look like? All she could picture was the ocean, teeming with thousands of waves. Surely if *she* couldn't make out a single wave in the sea, nobody out there could see her properly. She was just one person, lost in an ocean of people. It wasn't like the talent show, where the eyes of her schoolmates, teachers and parents would be on her alone. Besides, her *fantasia* disguised her.

Nina realized that she didn't have to be a perfect wave – she just had to do *something*.

She stopped trying to copy everyone else, and lifted her head to the lights. She felt the beat of the drums pounding through her body and tried to move to it. Her movements started to flow with the rest of the waves.

Occasionally she crashed into another girl, but she didn't let that bother her. She just kept going.

Nina's cloak sparkled under the lights. The feathers around her head fluttered. She left her thoughts behind and floated along, feeling as if she really *was* a little wave!

At the end of their performance, dancers took off their shoes and rubbed their feet. Musicians put down their instruments. The blue whale float was still once more. Nina was thirsty. Her arms and legs ached. She pushed through the crowd to look for Fernanda.

Nina wanted to admit that Fernanda had been right – being in the parade *was* fun! She had been able to wear a beautiful *fantasia* and forget about the Nina that her parents, teachers and friends expected her to be. For Fernanda, Carnival was probably an escape from her normal, everyday life too.

Now, however, the *fantasia* that Nina wore was making her hot and uncomfortable. Nina took off the cloak. The woman who had given it to her wasn't around, so she left it on an oyster shell and hoped it would be OK. She took off her *fantasia de cabeça*, and paused. It was very beautiful, and it fitted. Could this be her special *fantasia*? No. This *fantasia* could help her be like a wave, but it couldn't transform her into *anything* in the world. She put it down next to the cloak.

Nina couldn't find Fernanda anywhere, and she was still thirsty. She spotted an opening in a fence. On the other side, a street party was going on. Perhaps she could buy a drink there. Nina looked at her watch. She still had time before she had to meet Ronaldo and return to the shed.

Nina took one last look around for Fernanda, then hopped through the hole in the fence.

Chapter Eight

Nina weaved along the street. At every corner, different music played. Partygoers wearing a mix of costumes danced and laughed together.

People had brought televisions out onto the street. Nina glanced at one of the screens. The samba parade was being shown live on TV. It was another samba school's turn now. Princesses, frogs, wolves and a pumpkin-shaped carriage glittered under the lights. Nina guessed that their theme was fairy tales.

Smells of corn on the cob, fish, and bean fritters wafted towards Nina from stalls along the sides of the road.

"Hayal! Hayal!" said the people at the

stalls as she passed. She remembered hearing the same word at the beach. *Maybe it means "hello"*, thought Nina, and she started saying "hayal" to everyone she passed. Some people smiled. A few gave her funny looks.

She stopped at a stall piled high with green coconuts.

"Hayal," said Nina to the man at the stall.

The man at the stall nodded.

"Hayal," he said, and chopped the top off a coconut, put a straw in it, and handed it to Nina.

Nina took a five-real note out of her pocket and gave it to the man. He gave her four reals back.

She slurped the cool coconut water, then threw away the husk. Her time in Brazil was running out. She thought about her To Do list and frowned.

1. Find out more about Aunt Nishi's job.

She hadn't managed to do that.

2. Help Aunt Nishi.

She had failed at that too.

3. Find a special fantasia for my head.

Nina looked at all the *fantasias de cabeça*

around her. She would need a miracle to find her special *fantasia* here. It was like searching for a needle in a haystack – or a *fantasia de cabeça* in a *fantasia de cabeça* stack!

At that moment, a cluster of feathers parted to reveal a sign.

MAGIC BALL

at the
Copacabana Palace

That sounded promising. Where better to search for a special, magical *fantasia* than at a magic ball?

Chapter Nine

Nina sneaked past the doormen and into the Copacabana Palace Hotel, where the Magic Ball was being held. She felt as if she had slipped into a dream. Chandeliers twinkled, music played, and men and women in masks and feathers glided about the ballroom.

Nina gazed around. There, sitting on a chair at the other end of the ballroom – as if waiting for her – was a bejewelled, feathered headdress. It was special. Nina could feel it. It had to be the one that could transform her into anything in the world. She walked towards it, entranced.

It shone, as if made of pure gold. A row of

pearls encircled the bottom. Purple and gold feathers fanned out in every direction. Nina wanted to pick it up. But what if it belonged to someone else? Nina looked around.

Everyone else's costumes were complete. A man in a black-and-red mask appeared at the entrance of the ballroom and looked around as if searching for something, but Nina doubted this *fantasia de cabeça* had anything to do with him. It was far too beautiful, and he already had a mask. Madame Celeste had said that every single person had a special *fantasia*. Maybe this one was Nina's!

The only way to see was to test it out. She

picked it up. It was heavy. She lifted it to her head and put it on. It fitted! The power of the *fantasia* flowed through her.

She walked to the middle of the ballroom and started to dance. It was easy! Instead of feeling nervous and silly, she glided to the music like the elegant people around her. Yes, with this *fantasia* on her head, she had the power to become anything in the world . . .

GONG! The call to dinner vibrated through the ballroom. It was 19.00 hours! Nina was supposed to meet Ronaldo half an hour ago! More importantly, she was supposed to be back at the shed to meet Aunt Nishi this very minute. Nina spun round and bumped straight into the man wearing the black-and-red mask. What was he doing so close behind her?

"Sorry," she muttered as she dashed out of the Copacabana Palace Hotel. She hoped that Ronaldo was still waiting for her in front of the Sambadrome.

As she raced back towards the street party, Nina heard footsteps behind her. A few purple feathers from her *fantasia* came loose and floated away. Nina kept running.

The street party was now in full swing, and Nina had to squeeze through the crowds. The plumes on her headdress were pulled this way and that. Nina felt as if she was a bird, being plucked of its feathers.

She hopped through the hole in the fence and – RRRRRIP! Nina gasped. Her *fantasia* felt lighter and loose on her head. A bunch of feathers must have caught on the fence and been torn out. She couldn't bear to look back at the damage. Nina understood how awful Fernanda must have felt when her special *fantasia* was ruined. But if Fernanda could fix hers, perhaps Nina could do the same. The important thing was to get back to Aunt Nishi as soon as possible.

She made her way out to the front of the Sambadrome. There, she spotted Ronaldo's yellow taxi and ran over to it. As she got in and shut the door, she saw the masked man running through the crowd in her direction. He was looking left and right. *How strange . . .*

"Hayal!" said Nina to Ronaldo, happy to see him.

Instead of saying *Hayal* back, Ronaldo gave her an odd look.

Chapter Ten

"Oh no," groaned Nina as she sat in the back seat of the taxi. "I thought *Hayal* meant *Hello!*"

"Well, it can be confusing, because in Portuguese we pronounce the R as an H," explained Ronaldo as he sped up the mountain to the statue of Christ the Redeemer.

"That means I've been going around saying 'real' to everyone, which is like greeting people in England with 'pound'. And to top it off, I'm late!"

"No worries. Time slips away from everyone during Carnival!" said Ronaldo.

Nina hoped Aunt Nishi would see it that way too.

Ronaldo dropped Nina off at the bottom of the path, which was as far as cars could go.

"Thanks. You really are the best taxi driver in the world!" said Nina, giving Ronaldo a big tip and jumping out of the cab.

As she ran up the path, her *fantasia* kept slipping down over her eyes. A few more feathers floated away, but Nina had bigger things to worry about. Standing up ahead, with her arms crossed and brow furrowed, was Aunt Nishi.

As Nina approached, Aunt Nishi's expression changed from annoyed to confused, then surprised.

"I'm really sorry," said Nina, hoping she wouldn't get told off too much.

Aunt Nishi didn't respond. Her eyes were fixed on Nina's *fantasia de cabeça*. Was Aunt Nishi so angry that she couldn't even look at Nina? Or was she entranced by Nina's magical headdress?

Aunt Nishi lifted the *fantasia de cabeça* off Nina's head. Nina gasped when she saw it – almost all the feathers were gone! Only a few gold ones remained. Aunt Nishi began pulling them off. She was clearly punishing Nina for getting lost and being late.

"Aunt Nishi! Please, no! That's my special *fantasia*!"

"No it's not," said Aunt Nishi, pulling off the last of the feathers. "It's the Imperial Crown of Brazil!"

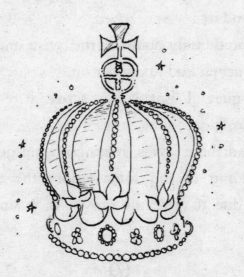

Nina looked at her *fantasia de cabeça*. Without the feathers, it *did* look like a crown. A crown made of solid gold, with jewels and a row of pearls encircling the bottom.

"But," said Nina, "it was a very beautiful *fantasia de cabeça* and it fitted and made me feel special, just like Madame Celeste said . . ."

"It was probably disguised to look like a *fantasia de cabeça*, because it was stolen from the Imperial Museum of Brazil earlier today! This is what I came here to look for, but I had failed to complete my mission – that is, until you came along. How on earth did you find it?"

Nina thought about all the twists and turns her journey had taken her on.

"I guess I just came across it – spontaneously!"

"And there I was, relying on my gadgets! According to my information, the thieves were due to give the crown to a smuggler

in Rio, and he was going to ship it out of the country. You must have picked it up at the exact time and place they had planned for the exchange!"

Nina thought about the man in the red-and-black mask. He must have been the smuggler, trying to get the crown off her! She shivered.

"I figured the swap should have taken place somewhere around the Copacabana Palace Hotel," continued Aunt Nishi.

"That's where I found it!" said Nina.

"Really? Then how . . . ?" Aunt Nishi inspected the crown. "Of course! I was so focused on searching for a crown that I didn't imagine it could be disguised as something else. Hundreds of feathers must have been stitched into the headband. No wonder it fitted your head so well. Of course, without all the feathers, it's too big," said Aunt Nishi, placing the crown over Nina's head to test her theory. "But you don't need a crown, Nina. You're already my little princess!"

Nina beamed. Not only was Aunt Nishi pleased with her, but Nina had ticked off two items on her To Do list. She had learned more about her aunt's job *and* helped out! But that meant she still hadn't found her special *fantasia* . . .

Chapter Eleven

Nina dragged her feet to school the next day.

It was Wednesday, and Nina still didn't know what she was going to do for the talent show. She had to talk to Madame Celeste.

She entered the school building. The sound of drums echoed through the halls. It grew louder as Nina approached the Music and Drama classroom. She knocked on the door but no one answered — the drums were too loud. Nina opened the door and peeked in . . .

Madame Celeste sat on the floor beating two small drums. Her bangles and beads shook, reminding Nina of the samba parade. Madame Celeste paused when she saw Nina.

"Sorry to disturb you, Madame Celeste, but I need to talk to you about the talent show," said Nina.

"Of course," said Madame Celeste.

"I don't know what to do. I mean, I could have been whatever I wanted if I had my special *fantasia*, but I lost it. Actually, I never really found it in the first place, I just thought I had . . ." Nina trailed off.

Madame Celeste looked confused. "Nina, what are you talking about?"

"The special *fantasia* you told me about. The one for my head. I thought I'd found it. It was beautiful, with purple and gold feathers – but then it turned out that it *wasn't* my special *fantasia* after all."

"Nina, the meaning of the word *fantasia* that I was talking about isn't 'costume', it's . . . what do you call it?" said Madame Celeste, clicking her fingers. "Ah! Imagination! The ability to become anything in the world by letting your mind wander free."

Nina couldn't believe it. She thought back to her conversation with Madame Celeste. She supposed Madame Celeste *could* have been talking about imagination. But what about Fernanda? She had a special *fantasia* without which she couldn't have danced in the samba parade. But maybe that was because she would not have fitted into the parade's theme. Maybe Fernanda meant that it was special in a different way. After all, she had been able

to dance just as beautifully without it when she was on her roof.

"You mean I've spent all this time and effort looking for some sort of special, magical *fantasia* which doesn't even exist?" asked Nina, feeling foolish.

"But you said you thought you'd found it, Nina. Tell me, how did it feel when you wore it?"

"Well, I suppose I felt free, like I could be anything in the world," said Nina.

"There you go! You really *did* find your *fantasia*! Because in that moment, you *imagined* that you were wearing something magical. It takes a powerful imagination to do that!" said Madame Celeste.

Nina had to admit that Madame Celeste was right. Her imagination had really taken flight in Brazil.

It was Friday, and the hall was packed.

Nina waited in the wings for Luca to finish juggling. Her heart pounded. She could see her parents and Aunt Nishi sitting at the back with the rest of the families. Her favourite teacher, Miss Matthews, stood to the right of the stage. Rows of children sat on the floor in front. Luca bowed, and everyone clapped.

Nina picked up her special *fantasia*. She had created it herself out of yellow, green and blue feathers, glitter and beads. She nodded to Madame Celeste, who was standing by the stereo system. Madame Celeste pressed play.

The sounds of samba vibrated though the hall, loud and exciting. Nina put on her *fantasia de cabeça*. The feathers around her head quivered. She left her worries behind, and danced.

About the author

Madhvi Ramani was born in London, where she studied English and then Creative Writing at university. Like Nina, she enjoys having adventures in different countries. She also likes blueberries, dark chocolate and books. She lives in Berlin with her husband and imaginary cat. You can follow her on Twitter @MadhviRamani.

Nina's Fantastic Facts about Brazil

☀ Brazil is the fifth largest country in the world.

☀ The Carnival in Rio takes place over several days, attracts millions of people and is often called "the world's largest party".

☀ The statue of Christ the Redeemer is 30 metres tall, not including its 8-metre-high pedestal. Its arms stretch 28 metres wide and it weighs 635 tonnes. That's one massive statue!

☀ Ronaldo is a retired Brazilian football player. He played for Brazil in 98 matches, scoring 62 goals, and is thought to be one of the greatest football players of all time.

☀ Samba is now a dance of Brazil, but its roots can be traced back to Africa.

☀ The tradition of Rio's carnival balls comes from Venice, Italy. The most famous of these is the Magic Ball at the Copacabana Palace Hotel.

Create your own Fantasia de Cabeça

(Make sure you have a grown-up to help you!)

You will need:

A headband
A long ribbon
Tape
Thick cardboard
Scissors
Paint
Glitter
Strong glue
A selection of beads and feathers (in whatever colours you like)

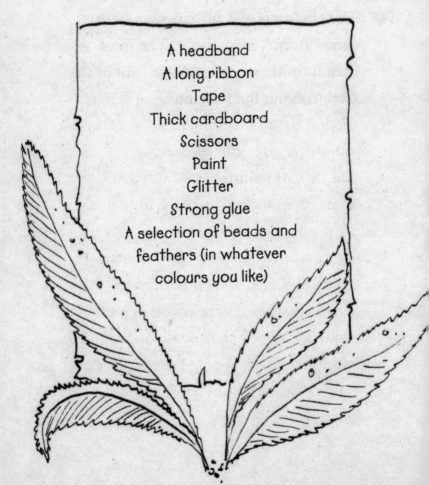

What to do:

Madame Celeste's tip: have fun, be creative — let yourself go!

1. Take the ribbon and loop it around your headband until it is entirely covered. Use some tape to fix the ends of your ribbon in place.
2. Cut the cardboard into different shapes — circles, squares, triangles, stars — all around 4 centimetres in size.
3. Paint the cardboard pieces different colours, then sprinkle them with glitter, and glue beads on.
4. Glue the shapes onto the front (outside) of your ribbon-wrapped headband.
5. Glue the feathers to the inside of your headband, so that they come up behind the shapes. You can glue feathers all the way around, or just along the middle section. It's up to you!

Join Nina on another globetrotting adventure!

Also available:

Nina and the Travelling Spice Shed

Nina and the Kung-Fu Adventure

'A promising new series which will help children learn about other countries and cultures' *Parents in Touch*